Flairs and Glairs
Publication House

"Seven Essence"

ISBN No: " 978-93-91302-31-3"
1st Edition
Language – English and Hindi

Flairs and Glairs
Publication House
Regd. Under MSME Act.

Disclaimer

This is a work of fiction and solely represent the thoughts of the corresponding authors of the articles. Our editors have tried their best to edit the content of all the authors and check the plagiarism.
All the write-ups in this book are unique and are only published in this book.
In case any plagiarism or error is found, only the author is responsible alone, and not the publisher or the Compilers.

Cover Designing and Book Formatting
Shubham Shah and Ishani Agarwal

Acknowledgement

Compiling this anthology was harder than we thought and more rewarding that we could ever imagine! Foremost we extend our thanks to the Great Almighty, the author of knowledge and wisdom, for his countless love.

This book is based on experiences, thoughts and ideas of many individuals, from far and near, who took an opportunity to be a part of this book. THANKYOU. dear co-authors for building a strong foundation for the anthology. Special gratitude to our family who supported me in the entire course and friends, Spoorthi HC, Twinkle Upadhyay, Ananya Mourya, Manya Devaraj for helping us reach many writers who wished to showcase their writing talents.

To all the relatives and friends, who in one way or other lend their helping hand for the completion of this work, we thank you! Concluding, by acknowledging, the readers, who will read this collection and inspire us to write even more. Last but most important, a ton of thanks to our publication "Flairs and Glairs", who showed immense faith in us and approved our chances to fulfil the dream of being a published author.

This anthology weaves the various life actions around the frame of alphabet C. It revolves around 7 C’s: Choose, Create, Change, Challenge, Concern, Chase, Close. Each of these verbs are interconnected at any point in life. As an example, for each step in the course of life, we either choose or create our path, which in turn has the power to change our future through ample number of challenges that it brings with it. We can tackle these challenges by simply having a concern towards our goal and chasing success with perseverance and that's how every task comes to an end or closes with a series of lessons and accomplishments. The co-authors have penned down their thoughts on either one or all of the C's, based on their personal experience or related notions in life.

This book covers the essence of these seven C’s in individual or collective manner.

Co Authors

Shubham Shah (Founder Flairs and Glairs)
Ishani Agarwal (Co-Founder Flairs and Glairs)
Sumit Sharma {Compiler}
Disha Devaraj {Compiler}

1. Mona Sundaram
2. Nidhi Khushhal
3. Gopika Gopinath
4. Harshith Rao
5. Sayanta Banerjee
6. Vishesh Saxena
7. Aditi Nahar Jain
8. Antim Engle
9. Athmika Bhat
10. Afifa Sharif
11. Yashaswini Un
12. Rakhi Gosain
13. Missa Mehta
14. Bhoomika
15. Shivani Prajapati
16. Aliya Khan
17. Spoorthi Hc
18. Sonia Edwina Joseph
19. Adarsh Pandey
20. Amit Pandit
21. Divas Vishwajna C
22. Nakshatra Mala Dash
23. Reynu (Shradha Shintre)
24. Samiksha Sharma
25. Raghav Chauhan
26. Ranajoy Biswas
27. R. Sagarikaa

28. Sonali Gouda
29. Simmy
30. Prashant Tyagi
31. Vishakha Malukani (Morika)
32. Sudipta
33. Ankit Acharya
34. Santosh Sharma
35. Manisha Shrivastava
36. Dr. Chandramani Goswami
37. Akhil Prakash
38. Chirag L Sagar
39. Niharika N Jain
40. Mariya Sadaf

Shubham Shah

(Founder- Flairs and Glairs)

Shubham Shah, an entrepreneur at "Flairs & Glairs" a brand with dynamics in events organizing and cultural educational pan INDIA, is a 26yrs old guy who recently has entered the digital platform of imprinting emotions. He has initiated with his own open mic platform to help budding poets and aspiring writers under his brand named as "Teekhe Zasbaaat"

He is a commerce graduate from the Bhagalpur City of Bihar. He states Writing has impersonated him since childhood and he has now been writing for over a decade!
Cooking, on the other hand, is his passion! He also mentions, trying out new things just tickles him!
When asked sir, Why SPICY EMOTIONS?
He smiled and added, "agar jasbaat teekhe na ho toh wo jasbaat kahan" Spices are all that blends! So do his words!
As a chef, he presents to you his dish! Hot and freshly served! Taste it! Feel it! Enjoy it! You can also find his writing in the Book "Teekhe Zasbaaat" and 50+ Co-authored anthologies. With his passion to explore opportunities across Platforms, he is working with keen devotion and We wish him all the very best for his future ventures.
He is Featured in the International Magazine DeMode for his upcoming solo novel.
He is Approved by Ne8x for its Lit Fest, and is a Golden Star Awards 2020 Winner.
He is a India Book of Records Holder for his Anthology Satrang, and has the Grandmaster title by Asia Book of Records, for the same.
He has also been featured in Prabhat Khabar, Dainik Jagran, and a lot of other Newspapers in Bihar for his achievements.
He has been a proud co-author to
India Book Of Records (Title- Black)
World Book Of Records (Title -15 Wonders of Poetries)
India Book Of Records (Title - Aaina)
Vajra World Records Holder (Title - Gustakhi Maaf Hai)
High Range of Records Holder (Title - Gustakhi Maaf Hai)
Indian Book of Records
(Title - Road from Worst to Best)

Share your reviews on his

INSTAGRAM

@spicy_emotions
@shubham4shah

Or via email on

shubham2shah@gmail.com

To stay tuned to his work and opportunities follow his business Handles

INSTAGRAM FACEBOOK YOUTUBE

@flairsandglairs
@teekhezasbaaat

WEBSITE:

https://flairsandglairs.in/
https://flairsandglairs.com/

Ishani Agarwal

(Co-Founder- Flairs and Glairs)

Ishani Agarwal hails from the City of Joy, Kolkata.
She is the co-founder of her Community "Teekhe Zasbaaat" and Flairs and Glairs Publication.
Been a Compiler for 45+ Anthologies, she is in the process for more. Co-authored in 150+ Anthologies. She is a India Book of Records Holder, a Vajra World Records Holder, a High Range of Records Holder, an OMG Book of Records Holder, a Bravo Record holder, a Forever Star Book of World Records and an Indian Book of Records Holder.
Approved by Ne8x for its Lit Fest 2020, and Literary Icon 2020. Also a Golden Star Awards Winner 2020.
She has also been awarded with India Star Republic Award 2021, a part of She Awards by Awards Arc and Winner of Nari Samman 2021 by Literoma.

She is also selected as Best Achiever of the Year by AwardsArc and Most Challenging Compiler Award by Spectrum Awards.
She got her first solo Published,a solo Compilation consisting of first 750 contents of hers, titled "Hand That Burnt While Healing".

She has been featured by the National Magazine "Taree Zameen Par" with the title 'unstoppable'.
Also featured in the International Magazine DeMode for her upcoming solo novel, she is proud to write on social issues, and is happy with the love she is receiving.
Connect with her on Instagram: @Ishani_agarwal_quotes / @compilations_so_far

Sumit Sharma

Sumit Sharma is published writer and compiler, Contributed in many anthologies. He hails from town of Madhya Pradesh named Ganj Basoda , belongs to Bhopal division. He is Attaining qualification in pharmaceutical sciences. *Elysian_an eye shower* is his first compilation of the year 2020. He is extremely fond of learning new things. He is versatile and believe in exploring self. Apart from writing he has keen interest in acting and dancing. ***The Radius, stuck on you*** are some of his compilations.

SCNEREY OF Cs

Bumble bees and butterflies,
Wandering on the flowers,
Choosing essence of their choice.
Some flies' feeds on food,
And then feeds on shit,
Why don't they choose,
What is right and where to fit?
This thought gives me a lesson,
Beauty speaks with the work and action.

Caterpillars turned adult,
Once walked with undulating waves,
Now are waving with air, they rise.
They rise, by the work they implicit.
They created a separate world for own,
Working on self for a period on count they are queen butterflies now,
Flying with the crown.

Blue sea seemed to be orange.
Clear sky turned to dark,
Shades of golden behind the mountains,
is of sun setting so far.
For few hours sedentary on the sore,
Capturing these colours,
Before it all shutters.
I was observing this view,
And want to capture it all.
And I conclude that changes are beautiful,
When it's for raise, not for fall.

Who cares for such little things?

The sun descends and will raise for sure!!
The Almighty have concern for this,
Okay.
But have you concern for own?

Changes are challenging though,
this says the night.
Buzz and business of the day,
is silent, I must seek for mine.

The sun which left the sky so dark,
Will raise high, the next day with same golden spark.
again, birds will chase the sky.
there is no closing of the events,
until you shutter your eyes.

If comes a pause then start again,
choose, create and Chase.
Change, Challenge will automatically arrive.
just have a concern, for your smile.
It should not be erroneous

Disha Devaraj

Disha Devaraj, the compiler of seven essence She is a writer from Sringeri, Karnataka with over 15+ anthologies published as co-author. Disha speculates that writing provides the best solace at all moments.

Chase the Crown

Take your own time to study hard
Fill your bank account to use anytime money card

Be busy in your own world
Let people feel you for a; feeling of proud

Chase your dream until your success scream
Get a schedule for day and night;
Create your own thoughts
So, get ready to fight

People must cheer; when they hear about your skills
Be valued to stay inspired

Be ready to do anything;
For your loved ones to keep happy;
Sorry move the word from your heart called "maybe"

Be ambitious,
To have a mind of curious,
And your own;
To wear an independent crown.

Mona Sundaram

Mona is a writer by passion. She writes by her pen name Blossom Mist. She gets inspiration from the most simple and at times even the most mundane things. She believes that everyone and everything is beautiful. She has published two anthologies. An avid reader, coffee and chocolate lover, loves to travel and cook. Apart from Instagram (@blossom.mist), you can contact her on Twitter(@BlossomMist).

एक पहिये की गाडी

कल बाज़ार में देखी
एक पहिये की गाडी
आड़ी तिरछी चल रही थी
कुछ मुश्किलों से लड़ रही थी
मैंने पुछा भैया इसे यूँ क्यों चलाते हो
मैंने पुछा भैया इसे यूँ क्यों चलाते हो
दूसरे पहिये को क्यों न लगाते हो
उस मज़दूर ने मुझे देखा और हंस पड़ा
कहा क्यों इस पर तंज़ कस्ते हो
अपाहिज है पर चल लेगी
एहम बड़ा है इसमें
दूसरे से न मिल लेगी
मैंने कहा इस निर्जीव को एहम में न तोलो
दूसरे पहिये से किस्मत का ताला खोलो
उसने कहा तुम्हें इस निर्जीव का एहम दिखता है
हम सब एहम के एक एक पहिये में चलता है
Empowerment, freedom, space, choice
ऐसा एक एक पहिया सब लिए फिरते हैं
न दूसरे से मिलते हैं
बस अकेले ही लड़ते हैं मेरी गाडी को छोड़ो
दोस्ती, समझ ,support और प्यार
ऐसे तुम अपना दूसरा पहिया जोड़ो
इस एक पहिये के समाज को फिर पूरा करके छोड़ो
ये बात सुन, मैं हैरान हुई
आइना देख कुछ परेशान हुई
अब मुझे यूँ एक एक पहिये दिखते हैं
जो दूसरे की तालाश में फिरते हैं चलो
अब हम लड़ना छोड़ें अपना दूसरा पहिया जोड़ें!!

Leave to Live

Stand Up and Move
No One Needs to Approve
It should be a choice
To finally hear the inner voice
No further you need to give
Be yourself, leave to live

Nidhi Khushhal

Nidhi Khushhal, She's NEET 2021 aspirant soon She'll be a medical student Currently She's residing in Indore "the cleanest city" She has a keen interest in writting. Other than this she is also interested in music (listening as well as singing). Her favorite writer is Gulzar Sahab, Faiz Ahmed Faiz, Waseem Barelvi, Nida Fazli and many more.

एक दर्द ऐसा भी

महीनों बाद पेन में लिपटी हुई स्याही जब कागज़ पर पड़ती है ऐसा लगता है जैसे आंखों में छिपाए गए आंसू आज चेहरे की सैर कर रहे हो॥ ऐसा लगता है जैसे कई सालों से किसी से बिछड़ने का गम झेल रही है जैसे सूख गई है वो, वो जैसे किसी की नजर लग गई है उसके नीले रंग को और लगे भी क्यों ना नीला रंग मन को भाता ही इतना है जैसे किसी ने उसे इतनी चोंट पहुंचाई हो कि आज शब्दों में बदलने से वो खुद को रोक नहीं पा रही हो जैसे कुछ एहसास चीख़-चीख़ कर बयां होने के लिए तरस गए हों॥ दर्द भी कुछ ऐसा मानो महीनों से बंद पड़े कमरे में पड़ी हुई टेबल की धूल हो जो निकाले ना निकलती, उसका हाल मानो तार पर पड़ी हुई पानी की उस एक बूंद सा हो जो बारिशों के बाद अकेलेपन से जूझ रही हो गिरने का सहारा ढूंढ रही हो॥ स्याही तो निमित्त मात्र है मैं तो अपना हाल सुना रही हूं, हां सही सुना आपने मेरा हाल..हम सब का हाल "एक दर्द ऐसा भी" - हां हम सब एक ऐसे दर्द से जूझ रहे हैं जो सिर्फ और सिर्फ हम जानते हैं, जिसके बारे में किसी को भनक तक ना हो और हो भी कैसे कभी कहा ही नहीं किसी से कभी महसूस ही ना होने दिया हो किसी को सिवाय पलंग पर पड़े हुए उस तकिए को जो आधी रात में बहाए गए तुम्हारे सारे आंसू सोखता है जो आंखों से गिरते हैं॥ वो बेजान बेज़ुबान चुपचाप मेरी कहानी सुनता है, कभी कोई सवाल नहीं करता बेशक हम सभी की कहानियां अलग-अलग हो सकती हैं पर दर्द एक से हैं किसी से बिछड़ने का दर्द, किसी को खोने का दर्द..किसी अपने को किसी बहुत खास को चाहे वह परिवार हो, दोस्त हो, मोहब्बत हो, चाहे वह कुछ भी क्यों ना हो, उससे हमारा चाहे कोईं रिश्ता ना हो, वह हमारा कुछ ना लगता हो, फिर भी उससे हमारा नाता हो, मन का नाता, भावनाओं का नाता, आत्मा का नाता॥ इन सब में से एक सबसे खास रिश्ता होता है, खून का रिश्ता जो मेरे दिलों दिमाग में हलचल मचा देता है, जो मुझे तार-तार कर देता है, मेरे सीने में दबी हुई आग को एक चिंगारी देकर

सुलगा देता है, इतनी ताबड़तोड़ मचा देता है मेरे हंसते खेलते जीवन में जैसे किसी भयानक तूफान के आ जाने से किसी का घर उजड़ गया हो, मेरे पैरों तले की ज़मीन मेरे स्पर्श से परे हो जाती है मैं निःशब्द, खामोश इस उम्मीद से उन लम्हों को टटोलने की कोशिश करती हूं कि काश मैं फिर से उन्हें जी सकूँ, जिन्हें मैंने जीना चाहा था जिन्हें मैं खोना नहीं चाहती थी पर अफसोस वक्त काफी आगे बढ़ चुका है कुछ इस तरह मानो उसके पहियों को किसी ने इतनी रफ्तार दी हो कि वो बस चलता ही जाता है, कहीं रुकता नहीं मैं चाहूं भी तो पीछे नहीं जा सकती॥ कहते हैं बीती बातों को सोचा नहीं करते पर क्या यह मन हमारे वश में है क्या? आखिर क्या किया जाए? हदों की हद से पार बेहद मैं हर वक्त सोचती ही रहती हूं॥ उस खयाल को कैसे भुलाया जाए यह भी तो उसी मुद्दे की बात है ना..फिर भी दिल पर पत्थर रखकर आगे बढ़ना होता है, अपने आप को हालातों के साथ साथ बदलना होता है, किसी को चुनना पड़ता है, किसी के खातिर किसी को खोना पड़ता है, बेमतलब की चिंता को छोड़ना पड़ता है, जीवन में आने वाली हर उस चुनौती को स्वीकारना पड़ता है जो हमें एक दिन आसमान की सबसे ऊंचाई पर ले जाएगी अर्जुन की तरह सिर्फ उस एक लक्ष्य के पीछे भागना पड़ता है जो उन सारे बुरे पलों के खयाल तक को भी एक झटके में रफा-दफा कर देगा अगर हम उस मंजिल तक पहुंच गए जहां हम जाना चाहते हैं और इसीलिए जिंदगी के पिछले पन्नों को या तो यूं कह लो कि उन सारे अध्यायों को बंद करना पड़ता है, एक बेहतरीन और खुशनुमा जीवन को जीने के लिए अपने हाथों से बनाना पड़ता है साफ शब्दों में ये कि उन सारी चीजों को भुलना पड़ता है जो दुखों का पहाड़ बनकर सामने खड़ी हो जाती हैं॥ यही तो है ना जिंदगी?? भूलना पड़ता है ,सहना पड़ता है, जीना पड़ता है॥

Gopika Gopinath

Gopika Gopinath was born and brought up in Mysore, India. She received her bachelors of engineering degree from the VTU Belguam. She is currently working for an IT company in Banaglore. We could say she is an Engineer by day and a writer by night, Apart from writing, Gopika spends most of her time reading. She currently lives with her newly wed husband. You can chat with Gopika on instagram at @gopika_gopinath

Chosen Path

I inhale the scent of jasmine flowers as I set the table in my garden. These plants were the only thing keeping me going nowadays. I Planted and nourished them. The white flowers covered every inch of the plant making a floral fence along my compound. Roses of different colours placed here and there Which looked highlighted between the Jasmines. The lawn was neatly made. I covered the Garden table with the Blue Tablecloth and arranged four chairs.

The house help brought me tea in a teapot and placed it on the table. I sat down like I would for the past three years watching the gate from my seat, yet today was different. There were four cups instead of one on my table and there was a smile on my husband's face. The smile I had fallen for all those years ago, it was the most beautiful thing. I thought I would never see this day in my lifetime. The smile had faded away when Rohit went away, leaving us behind choosing his dream against our will. Kumar was heartbroken and our daughter Nidhi was the one who faced all his wrath. She had a month left to graduate but Kumar forced her to take over our Resort Business. The Summer season was full of tourists and she was still new in the field. She would work until late in the evenings and come home to a disappointed father who told here how worst she was at work and how bad life will be for her if she fails to graduate. She would hide inside the bathroom and cry later at night.

The man I married was full of compassion, but he was lost in his own sorrow to realize he had no right to decide what our children wanted to do. This continued for three months after which Nidhi couldn't take it anymore. She simply told him she was the Manager and she would take care. The resort was renovated as per her likings and business picked up. She became the apple of his eye. He would proudly brag about her achievement with friends. She never really spoke to him and he didn't apologize. After six months we had received a letter from Rohit telling he was posted in Secunderabad and would know more once he reports there. I was proud of him. He was a brave soul from childhood. He always fought for what he wanted, this time the price was his father's affection.

My two beautiful children one chose to leave and the other chose to listen. At the end they lost the precious bond with their father. Kumar was so determined to see Rohit take care of his assets he was blind to see how well Nidhi took care of it, neither did he notice how happy Rohit was with all his achievements at the army. I now understand the meaning of happiness being a state of mind. I saw the Grey i10 park in front of our gate as Kumar yelled in excitement "They are here!". I saw Rohit run towards me as I got up, he hugged me "Hi Ma! How are you?" he asked. "Never better" I said as a tear rolled out of my eye. Nidhi sat down and I saw Kumar pour a cup of tea for her. He had never done that before.

We soon settled down and grabbed our tea. Kumar cleared his throat. "I Noticed that i haven't been myself for the past couple of months but today i know that you were right Meera" He told looking at me. Nidhi raised an eyebrow while Rohit leaned forward to listened to him. I smiled. Kumar looked at them and continued ,"The day you chose to apply for the job at the Army, I was so furious and your mother told me when I had given a chance to reject our arranged marriage if she didn't like me. I should give you a chance to reject our Resort for your dream." Rohit exclaimed "I dint know that!". "I didn't listen to her; I became the villain in your sister's life instead. I dumped all the responsibilities on her without giving her any training on how to work while she was supposed to enjoy with her friends. But she never argued unlike you. I know I was wrong, I'm sorry" Said Kumar as he patted on her back.

I leaned back in my chair and captured the perfect family reunion. Our life will let us walk different paths; some we are asked to take while the others we chose to take. Not everyone will be happy with this. When given time some realize and re-joins your journey, and some departs and never look back.

"I never expected that" Rohit said. There was a hidden hope in his voice. The tiny little wish in his heart which would never come true. Sanjana was a sweet girl, they did love each other but they wanted different things in life. She wanted to marry him but not a soldier, but he wanted to be one. I smiled at him. The hope vanished but his smile remained.

Harshith Rao

Harshith.g.s.rao, I'm a 2nd year puc student studying at jyothy kendriya vidyalaya banglore. My hobbies are usually writing poetry in my mother tongue, wacthing movies and cooking for my family. Basically, my area of interest is writing stories and scripts. But writing articles was my first experience. My ambition is to be a best story writter and director. Already my two of the stories are been ready but due to my education I have kept it aside. I always believed that writing articles is like cooking a sweet, which is prepared with so much of interest but has a limit to have it. Writing is the only way for relaxation. For a poet everything around him is a beauty and can see many amazing things around them. And I'm one of them. Instagram: @harshith__Rao__

Challenges For Life

This life is so beautifully designed by a creator, who does not reveal his appearance or voice but his works are mighty. He has given a life for a soul and sent from heaven all the way to earth through a womb of goddesses. He has given everything to live happy on this planet. But we humans always expect more than what is needed and this is titled as "greed". This life is a game of life and death. It's a challenge by creator to we humans saying do or die. "Challenge", it's a salt of every meal. A life without challenges faced are food without salt in meal. As much as salt plays important role in adding the taste in food, challenge add taste for your delicious life of meals. These challenges are like father for us because, it is so rude in behaviour but always try to make us independent and strong as a dad make. We ignore challenges sometimes but once the opportunity is lost, recreations is only way out. Challenges for life is not a burden, instead it's a praise to us from mighty creator to improve or grow our graph of life. We humans as explorer should always be taking up new ideas, new works and new initiatives, on this long way we face many obstacles, ups and downs and problems. As everyone says every problem have a solution, it's not so easy to find solutions for problem as it says. It needs a huge dedication, confidence and a heart to complete the given challenge. Sometimes, in the way of finding a solution or dealing with our challenges fails couple of times, where it would be almost done and only a few steps away would be our goal. After twice or thrice failures also we must not die in this game. As much as we fail, we build ourselves stronger than before. This challenge makes ourselves and our lives stronger every time. It is the only thing which makes us to build ourselves, our confidence and our future. Nothing will go with flow as a carefree people

says. Everything has its own time, own place and own Level of struggle to get it. As we were in the age of toddlers walking on our legs were our challenge. As we grow still more older, eating by our own was our challenge. Getting still more older, we were admitted to a babysitting and living without parents half a day was our challenge and we were used to it. As we went to full day school, nobody cared us as much as before. We must eat, walk and write it's a challenge. As we grow still more older in teens many wrong ways infuse us and not getting into it is challenge. likewise, in particular ages the life throws a challenge on us. These challenges must be taken as a game and to be played with a sportive manner. Challenge will not come with an invitation before saying its arrival. It's like a direct "check" for a king in chess. King must be saved by our talent, with use of crew before "checkmate". We must be ready for everything at any time. A virus which infects human and Couse death and doesn't have any anti-body and this so-called corona virus was a great challenge to government of not only our nation but most of the nation all around world. Suffering of people, helplessness of doctors created a huge devastation for human life as well as economy. This is a challenge faced by government, but as it is big problem our honourable prime minister every time tries to deal it in a cooler way with lots of patience. This is what a person needs while dealing with a problem or challenge. Challenges are best friends they be cruel; they be a best teacher and best moment of life. Each and every one is talented equally but not same. As a human being one must surely go through the challenges, let's take challenges for life as best friend and best teacher. This makes us to walk in streets of success... " Challenges are to build ourselves, our confidence not our fear, trust in oneself and self-respect".

Sayanta Banerjee

Sayanta is an electronics and communication engineer who has a passion for writing and literature. He loves creativity and art. He believes that helping someone is the biggest work that you can do in a lifetime. And he also believes that weilding a pen is more powerful than that of a sword as it can make smile or rain tears at the same time.

Dream

He saw it in night, coming along spreading it's wings;
Like an angel bestowed in sight,
making him swing hard on the flings.
Above he goes with it, defying the odds;
The more he approaches, he never saw any lauds.
Criticism clouds his way, making his efforts seem like rust;
Dusty iron ore shines brightly with success profounding a crust.
Never he thought,
his family members will squash him with deploration;
Better he got to see the masked sentiments with defibrillated coloration.
Readied himself for a battle with the society,
he marched on keeping the dandelion;
Relatives busied on keeping him down with nefarious jobs ended with futile abortion.
An act of aggression,
with a bit of suppression totalling and doubling down on repression fighting depression;
Sought a degree for a mighty transgression and challenged a capitalist migration.
With all plighting efforts in his heart and conspicuously astounding brilliance in his mind, he made a scream;
But all he showed everyone a picture of how to not let go of your dream.

Vishesh Saxena

He is Vishesh Saxena from Jhansi pursuing b.tech (CSe) from Dehradun. His passion is drawing go and follow up his insta arts_legend_

I

I choose you from the crowd of millions of hearts,
I gave you opportunity to choose to weather to die,
on my chest or alone in this world of darkness.
you were worthless,
you were useless,
you were hopeless,
but I choose YOU still because I love you,
so I never replace I changed you,
and changing you means changing my life.

I do still remember
those moments created by you for us,
I do still remember
the heart full of happiness created by you for me,
so now I want to create the world filled with your wishes,
filled with my love, filled with lights,
so now I want to create poetry in you,
I want to build the world of happiness in fix it in your heart

this I promise to you that I'll never leave you,
the place of yours will never change in my life,
because changing your heart in my life,
will destroy me for you I can change your surroundings,
for you I can change myself, but I'll never change your
place in my heart.

yes I scold you, sometimes shout on you but,
i do for you because I am concern about you,
i am concern about you that much because i don't
want to lose you from my life, as oxygen is needed to
breath
same as you are my oxygen you are my life to me.

loving you is my challenge,
making your standing in society is my challenge,
saving you from darkness is my challenge,
protecting you from bad visions is my challenge,
because loving you in my biggest challenge.

I love you from my true heart,
so ill chase you till your grave,
ill chase you till you become mine,
chasing doesn’t means troubling you,
my chasing means I need you because I love you.

love is stronger,
if we are closer to each other's heart,
when I close my eye, I imagine you,
your smile,
your essence,
your hairs in the air,
your pleasant vibes,
all projected on my mind when I close my eyes
last wish of mine is please do be with me,
because I love you and want to close my eyes on your laps
on your laps....

Aditi Nahar Jain

She's an aspiring writer who lives vicariously through her words. An introvert, collector of pens, who spends most of her time with coffee and books; searching the path to Alchemy of words and language of Universe. An orator, who ironically believes in staying silent and letting her writings speak.

Selfish Tale of Selfless Love

Choose
Happiness over me
Because I will be prioritizing
My peace over you.

Create
A world of Reality
My wonderland will intoxicate
The living world out of you.

Change
The perspective of your mind
The glass is not always half empty or full
But sometimes, broken and shattered.

Concern
About the oblivion
It should not drive you towards insanity
The Waters of Lethe is not meant for taste.

Challenge
Yourself to be a better version of you
Because I won't hold your hand to the path of perfection
That's your road to walk.

Chase
Your ambitions instead of me
I'd be running away from the unsatisfactory chore
Chasing myself over you.

Close
The melancholic door of your bleeding heart

You need to fill your cup before you pour
When it's time, fate will bind us together till eternity and forevermore.

Antim Engle

Poetry is not a language but its the reality.... Antim Engle is a schooling girl studying in 11th standard .She believes in "Inhale the reality and Exhale the poetry."

“होंसला"- जिंदगी से बडा़ है।

होंसला जिंदगी से बडा़ है,
ख्वाब चांद तारे ये खुला आसमां है,
इन दिवारो से निकल कर
शहर से कहीं दूर जाना है,
हर चुनौती को छु कर गुज़र जाना है।

होंसला जिंदगी से बडा़ है
तिर पर क्यु रुकु,
मुझे तो लहरों को ललकारना है,
बहुत जी लिए इन अंधेरी रातों को
अब अपना आफ्ताब बुलाना है
हर चुनौती को छु कर गुज़र जाना है।

मंजिल तो मिलेगी भटक कर हि सही
फिर घर में बेठी यु गुमराह क्यु रहू।
इस खेल खेलती जिंदगी को
अपना खेल दिखाना है।
सच्चाई को नहीं अपने सच को दिखाना है।
कल रोता छोड़ आई थी जिंदगी को,
उसके लिए आज कुछ करिश्मा कर जाना है।
हर चुनौती को छु कर गुज़र जाना है।

Athmika Bhat

A communicator by profession and bibliophile by passion, Athmika loves to use words to connect with the world.

Fleeting Days of Childhood

A small step, a baby cry
Into the world with a lot of smile
A jump, a fall and wounds dry
In all a villain and docile
Stepping in a bright day
It's a beginning, a new way
All the lessons, a fresh say
Numerous pranks if permission may

The beauties of childhood
And unaccountably many too
All the games, colours, dress and food
Fun times in the beach and zoo

If I were to let back now
To go back, to my childishness
You may doubt it how
But do not forget the evergreen freshness

Life starts then with a vision
Hoping that is realised
As we grow, we drive into mission
We let our parents make us biased

That playful child in me I forgot
In this world of strife and maturity
I beg you to remember the lessons taught
In divine childhood with trust and security

The Peaceful War

The blast from a cannon den
The march of soldiered men
The silence of a landmine
The distant warning of a war whine

Battlefields and stream of bloodshed
Carcasses and decay wed
This glorified battle of pride
Leaving scars and wounds open wide

Then comes the rain floating down
To soothe frayed nerves and constant frown
Bringing time to build and gain
The life that was lost, yet again

Keep the peace and keep the calm
Light the lamp, be a soothing balm
The wound ought to cover and heal
With it, the nightmares seal

We look constantly outward
For the brave and the coward
But the struggle yet continues
In our mind with emotion cues

Bring peace onto yourself
Leave the burden on the shelf
A war need not be violence
Said Mahatma, come back to your sense

Work your way to the rightful fight
Fits and sticks, out of sight

Take to peace and powerful silence
Jump in the swadeshi fence

Make the pen mightier than the sword
Task the mind higher than the body board
Truth and non-violence, a silent strike
Push Satyagraha, the righteous spike

The peaceful war - the way to go
The right seed for one to sow
Becoming the tree which reaches the sky
Allowing all to spread and fly

War and peace try to work its way
The peaceful war is here to stay!

Afifa Sharif

Afifa Sharif, born and brought up in Patna, Bihar. Currently she is pursuing BA (Hons) in English from Amity University, Lucknow campus. She loves to read and write poetry. She is also interested in different genres of literature from Middle age to post modernism through Gothic, romantics, feminism, fantasy and many more. She is a dynamic lady with her writings. Apart from this, she is an imaginator in her real life as well as expert in intellectual works. Afifa never fails to motivate others through her word. You can catch her vibes on instagram @irresistible_._phoenix as well as on twitter Afifa Shariff.

I Found Myself.

I went in search to know,
What the universe is?
Ah! Now look,
I'm here,
Standing with a question;
Who truly am I?

I left my nest to get best,
Now, I feel like whatever I have, is the best.
I left my home,
To explore from east to west
Now, my own place seems to be the best from the rest.
I want everything to be perfect,
Now, I am having the best intellect.
The only thing,
I'm craving for is 'REAL'.
In the process to heal
I'm standing without any fear.
I can be everything or,
I can be nothing.
Because, I know,
What I'm now.
I'm everything I ever wanted to be,
Finally, I found 'me',
I'm the universe and the universe is me.

I Raised My Range

I walked down memory lane,
Those hurdles were like hurricane,
And I stood there on a cellophane,
So, I raised my range.

I wasn't ready to make change,
Nor, I wanted to be in a cage,
I couldn't put myself in a downrange,
So, I raised my range.

I was on a rollercoaster of my life,
I set myself for a long drive,
To be a warrior and to keep myself alive,
So, I raised my range.

I raised my range,
To see mircles around.
I raised my range,
To win all the battleground.
I raised my range,
To not to be a puppet of a Clown.
I raised my range,
And now you'll see me in a crown.

Yashaswini UN

Yashaswini from chikkamagalur. She did her graduation in Mechanical engineering. Loves to do Painting, Pencil sketch, and following passion is what she likes

Make A Change

Chase your stars fool
Life is short
Create a spark
Ignite the Envies
Choose your path
And never Regret
Change on your own
Make sure to reach your goal
Because life is short
And life goes on
Chase yourself
In all the blues
And I will be with you
In all your Grey's
Take out the best of you
And Make a change

Rakhi Gosain

We would like to introduce Rakhi Gosain as a new author in the town. She loves writing Life Quotes and Poems in fiction. Mirror Talk (Each Question Has A Different Voice) is her first published poem (in fiction) in an Anthology named "Unvoiced Words" and now she is working with us as a Co-author in our new project "Seven Essence". She believes that writing is the best way to kick the stress out from your life even when a pandemic tries to turn everything shut down and she says "writing gives you a stage where you can set your thoughts free to dance and speak candidly."
We wish her Good Luck for her upcoming undertakings.
Instagram: @myflyingnotes
Email: gosain.rakhi92@gmail.com

Smile Over Pain

One random day, I started getting flashbacks,
glimpse of memories, where I saw a lost version of mine,
A version, where there is a body but have no life and spine.
I looked so shocked and worried,
and folks played well to make me feel scurried.

I found myself drowning in the stream of sympathy and pity,
I weeped, rubbed my eyes before it gets more gritty.
Then, when I came back to my senses I sensate that this is not the life I've ever dreamed about,
No,no, no...! no matter what season I'm breathing in...no seed of sorrow I will let sprout.

So what If I lost the game once more
I will always choose to keep my loss at shore,
I will choose smile over pain and get my strength back
And I will choose to step up again if I ever fall off track.

In Search of a Pearl

I woke up this morning sat beside my window
and raised my palm to wipe the window glass

and
I saw a girl collecting sea shells,
She looked insane when filling up her pail.
Like she wanted to grab all the good things at once,
Like she was dying to live all the levels of life without any fail.

Every time when she saw an oyster shining,
Sea waves tried to cover it up with the sand.
And wishing good luck for her I was enjoying that scenery,
With a mug of hot coffee in my hand.

The waves kept coming and going,
Maybe they are testing her fortitude.
But the girl was so sure that she's gonna chase,
So, she didn't stop smiling and considered it all a platitude.

She was determined that she will find what she has come for,
Neither there was a fear of storms nor of a whirl.
She started removing sand and kept digging with a toy shovel,
In a hope that she will certainly get a pearl.

Missa Mehta

MISSA MEHTA, from Bhuj-Kutch-Gujarat. She graduated with bechelors degree in English Letrature in year 2020. She likes to write poem at her own view. She likes to travel and from that she explores her writting capacity. She took part in several anthologies. She writes many poem,articles and motivational stories.

instagram: @anubhav_nu_aakash
Gmail: missangelmehta17@gmail.com

Be The Best Creator

Your abilities show your future life,
You're the best painter of your life.
Your confidence is only game changer,
You're only one who is your supporter.
You're on your journey of searching,
Complete the goals without over thinking.
May you feel your mind has limits,
Your body & soul is free from limits.

Nothing Is Constant

Nothing is constant in this World,
Not even troubles,joys and relations.
"Change"everything is in a one word.
Everything comes to teaches lessons.

You are on your journey of life,
Meet so many people during this time.
Everything is possible-take it right,
There are so much golden waiting light.

If you want,for it ;you have to fight.
To become superstar, you've to write.
Rule i.e. the game you never quit.
In this limitless role,you have to fit.

O Dear!Be your biggest supporter.
B'cause you're marvelous creator.
It's okay to take time for yourself.
But always listen your inner self.

Never allow to change your mindset,
People are ready to change other's live.
Maintain your relation which you get.
Hold their hands and enroute's life.

Bhoomika

Bhoomika is an overthinker, previously used it to ruin herself but now to build herself she want her writings to reach most of the people so that they think " oh! she is not the only one like this " And her main intention is to spread some love and positivity through her writings.

Choice

I chose you over everyone and everything,
But your priorities were different,
I agree, not your mistake but not mine too,
You had a lot of responsibilities, you added me as one too,
But I wanted to be your support and not burden,
Yes, now.... I chose myself and my mental peace over everyone and everything.

Create

I believe that we create our life,
based on our thoughts.
But I didn't know that thought can affect so much,
That it can change one's life from nothing to everything,
May be even vice versa!

Shivani Prajapati

Shivani Prajapati is a student and she loves writing inner thoughts in forms of story and poems.

Fear of Dream

I have a dream, I have a goal, I have a big carrier,
and I want to catch that dream of mine, goal of mine,
I want to reach at the top whatever it takes.
But there is a path between us, a big and a difficult path.
I have to pass through that path where I will be meeting lots of emotions,
difficulties, hard times, problems.
I have a lot of confidence that one day I will be at the top.
I really don't believe in luck, I only believe in hard work
and I know one day my hard work will bring success. But......
I am losing my confidence little by little,
whenever I am taking one step forward on life's stair,
my legs start to shake, I feel like I will fall from the stairs.
My legs are shaking just like two years old child.
I will be going to fall or maybe I will give up on my dream
if there will be no support.
I want a support if it will be from behind, from front, from besides,
I will take that support, but how can I take someone support,
everyone has their own path, stairs to travel, so why they will support me.
I can move forward all alone while watching others.
My feelings of happiness are wavering, I am scared,
day by day fear of falling spreading in my body rather than happiness
just like some incurable disease.
This incurable disease is blocking my path.
What will happen if I can't able to remove these blocking?
What if I lose all the confidence?
What if I can't able to reach at the top?
What if I can't able to catch my dream?
What if I can't able to travel that path?
What if I have a big disease?
What if next day I die...............?

Unpredictable Life

If you want whole world,
to listen your story.
Just show them the life's theory.
If you want to gain
attention of everyone,
then just burn like a sun.
If you want happiness,
just face every sadness.
Because life is so beautiful,
you don't want to see,
how it is wonderful.
Be yourself, be a crazy,
and life will be too much easy.

Aliya Khan

Aliya Khan, writes poetry, which, considering where you're reading this, makes perfect sense. She is best known for her poetry, hindi shayari and small write ups on life. She is a teacher by profession and currently living abroad in the UAE. She hails from the city of Mumbai where she completed her Bachelors in Commerce before she went abroad to pursue her Masters qualifications and settled there. To read more of her write ups you can visit her blog on Instagram @poetry_byak.

अनकहे एहसास

ना वो मेरी तकदीर में है
ना मै उसकी किस्मत में!
ना जाने फिर क्यों यह दिल उसे अपना बनाने की कोशिश में रहता है!

तेरी आगोश में कुछ वक्त मिल जाए,
सारी उम्र उस ही लम्हे में कट जाए,
तू करीब हो और क्या चाहिए ?
तेरे लम्स से शायद इस दिल को सुकून मिल जाए....

गिला भी तुझसे बहुत है मगर,
मोहब्बत भी है इस कदर...
वो बात अपनी जगह है,
और यह बात अपनी जगह!

तुमको भूल जाऊं,
यह मेरे बस में नहीं!
तुमको पा लूं..
ये मेरी किस्मत में नहीं!

तुम्हारी चाहत में शारिक ए मुकम्मल होने की दुआएं मांगा करते हैं..
ए जन ए ग़ज़ल,
पाया ही कब था ऐसे तुम्हे , जो अब खोने से डरते है ?

चलो मान लिया के तुझसे इश्क मेरे बस में नहीं ...
लेकिन मेरे साथ जो हुआ क्या वो था सही?
तेरी आदत लगी..

मेरी उम्मीदें बढ़ी...
फिर तू बदला, तेरी वफाएं बदली..
और मैं फिर एक बार रह गई अकेली।

तेरे इश्क से महरूम हम भटके दरबदर
मंज़िल तो तुम ही थे ना जाना, लेकिन तुम्हें कहां थी खबर?
तुम ना मिले अब यह दुनिया छोड़ चले हम
मानो ना मानो हमारे लिए कई आंसू बहाओगे सिर्फ तुम!!

औरों से जोर्ध के दर्जे में हमें तूने जो गिरा दिया।
लगा सीने में खंजर किसी ने बड़ी ज़ोर से चुभा दिया।

जब ज़माने की ठोकरें खाओगे तब हम पर यकीन लाओगे?
जाओ देख लो तुम भी सनम, दीवाना हमसा कहीं नहीं पाओगे!

Spoorthi H C

Spoorthi H C is a writer from Chikkamagaluru, Karnataka with over 30 anthologies published as a co-author. She began writing while still a student and aspires to be a full-time writer someday. She is a classical singer and dancer. By profession, she is an engineer but by passion, she is an expressive writer. She also writes in Kannada and has her work published in various newspapers and magazines from time to time. She also publishes her Kannada poetry on Instagram @kavithegala_saalu and her English poetries on @narrowsea_stories. An optimistic, unique individual with an infectious smile and a generous heart. Spoorthi assumes that words provide the best comfort at all times.
Recently she awarded "Nammura Nakshatra" state award for her contribution to the literature field.

Challenge The Challenges...!!

Bad days will occur,
Bad days will disappear,
If they are the best teacher,
Then absolutely I'm a decent learner.

Already, I dipped into those,
Unusual horrible circumstance,
Evaluated my inner courage,
Eliminated that unwanted cowardice,

I assembled my enthusiasm,
Get seized from that scepticism,
Day by day I gazed for optimism,
That changed my mannerism.

Yes! I challenged the challenges,
Celebrated those harsh sufferings,
Thrived there with visions and missions,
Finally, I'm here with my ambitions.

You're In My Poetic Lines!!

Walking on a wooden bridge,
Found it was calm and peaceful,
But my heart uttered with a love,
Oh, dear! Why are you dull??

Surrounded by amidst nature,
I Skipped all my failure and pressure,
Suddenly, I found his absence,
Couldn't even remember that!

Neither love nor care,
Nothing I have to except,
Because our priorities have changed,
We moved to an extended World!

That endless support and talks,
Now replaced with great silence,
Our delightful junctures and days,
Now rewritten in my poetic lines.

Sonia Edwina joseph

She hails from vizag, an elementary school teacher, she volunteers at a visually challenged community, she is a calligrapher and a water color artist.She is a poet who indulges in contemporary love and Gothic fiction genres.

Promise

I carved a piece of the night sky
Holding it between my palms
I gazed at it wishing
for a million stars to adorn that
chaos of neon emissions piercing up high
Some promises are delicately laced
And others remain tightly woven
Both inch towards a catastrophic end
Where promises fade like stars
Collapsing upon the wink of dawn.

Dandelions

We are all dandelions
With
Impossible wishes and dreams
We are sometimes overlooked
And most of the time scattered by the furious winds for
We are all dandelions
With
Impossible wishes and dreams
We bear someone's annoyance
While
Others miracle mantra
We are dandelions
With
Impossible wishes and dreams
We compose someone's most beautiful wishes to unfold
But
Others fierce dreams to be told
We are all dandelions my friends
With holding
Impossible wishes and dreams.

Adarsh Pandey

This is Adarsh Pandey belongs to Prayagraj, Uttar Pradesh, lives in Mumbai Maharastra. Adarsh is a author specializing in science – fiction and fantasy.. His website is www.writeradarshpandey.com

His published books are:

1. अच्छे निर्णय कै से लें(part1)
2. अच्छा निर्णय कै से लें(part2)

He contributed in the book The Radius as a co-author.

कोशिश

कल आज से बेहतर होगा ,
तू जरा कोशिस तो कर।
असफलता को सफलता में,
बदलने की कोशिश तो कर ।।
कष्ट के दिन बीतेंगे,
तू ज़रा कोशिश तो कर।
हाथों की चन्द लकीरों को,
बदलने की कोशिश तो कर।।

Today I Will Hear Everything

Listen to the traitors of the country, even today there are people who run on justice.

Even today the law runs on justice and supports the truth.

When some thieves and gentlemen of the country or officials of the government get reformed yet some people in our country have been victims of frost leaders or frost officers.

Today India is talking about how long there will be injustice to people, asks India, The government's job is to serve the public, to end the suffering of the people.

The job of the government is to protect society and the country rather than to create it.

In which case there are some people of India today who have not got justice yet.

Who should get justice why is injustice being done to him, the whole India asks. The injustice that has happened to the poor people so far and what is happening does not remain at the time of eclipse.

Do not force the mother of India so much that the people of traitors should expel you from this country.

The way India is witnessing injustice to people.

The day the pot of sin will be filled, the day it will be broken, listen to the pitcher, country men, I am the voice of India...

Amit Pandit

Amit Pandit belongs to Bhopal (MP). He is an Electronics & instrumentation engineer and works as a Power plant Automation Engineer at Sagar Group. His hobbies include writing Poetry, Poetry and Poetry. He is a published poet. "He contributed in the books titled The Radius, Melting Hearts and many as a co-author"

अहसास पन्नों में लिख लिए कविता बन गई,
और लिर प्रेम भी तन एक अनहि कल्पना ही है.!

तो क्या होगा !

अश्क़ अब्सार बन जाएं तो क्या होगा
सारे ग़द्दार बन जाएं तो क्या होगा ,

एक हमीं हैं जो हक़ीक़त पे यकीं रखते हैं
हम भी अख़बार बन जाएं तो क्या होगा.||

आंखों को आवाज़ बनाना पड़ता है
बहरों को भी शेर सुनाना पड़ता है,
हर मंज़र काग़ज़ की बहती कस्ती सा
पानी में भी आग लगाना पड़ता है,

जिन गलियों से काम नहीं है हमको पर
उन गलियों में आना जाना पड़ता है,
जिन लफ़्ज़ों का अर्थ नहीं ज़्ज़बातों में
उन लफ़्ज़ों का अर्थ बताना पड़ता है,

हर मौसम बादल की एक सच्चाई है
धरती को भी प्यास बताना पड़ता है,
जो लोगों को ख़्वाब दिखाया करते थे
उनको भी अब ख़्वाब दिखाना पड़ता है!

Divas Vishwajna. C

Divas Vishwajna. C who is a student of Aeronautical engineering Diploma. He lives in Bangalore but basically he is from Chikmaglure . He loves traveling and writing is his biggest strength.

Breathing On Death Desk

200 years ago, Saris the strongest soldier was teaching his 12 years old daughter Sara the lessons of courage. He did this by taking her to the forest and leaving her alone. She used to cry all the time. One day Saris sat beside her and took a deep breath, all of a sudden, a king cobra bit his leg twice. Saris knew that he will be dead in minutes, his daughter was fully blanked, he called Sara and took her forehead to his and said,

Saris: - Hey kid, don't cry.! You are a brave girl.

Sara: - Please Dad don't ever leave me...! (Sobbing)

Saris: - No my daughter, I am not leaving you.

Sara: - but the snake just bites you.!

Saris: - No, I'll be fine take this sword (slowly shutting his eyes)

Sara: - Pappa...! (Screaming)

As Sara completed her words Saris fell dead on the ground. Sara started to cry in pain beside her Father's dead body. After few hours, a pack of wolves arrived there because of the smell of the dead body. The wolves were happy by seeing Sara. Even she saw the wolves and she was blank with thousand question about her life after her father's death. A wolf bit her arm. She picked up the sword and cut off the head of the wolf, the head went rolling towards the other wolves, and the rest of the companions started to attack her.

She fought with all wolves and took her father's dead body with her towards her village. Thousands of memories sliding back-to-back her tears started to touch the ground. As she was carrying, her brain flashed (that the 1st wolf was their companion, even there companion was dead they never thought a second and they started to attack me) after she reached her village. It was attacked by some army and all the people were fallen dead. She fell unconscious after seeing her mother and brother dead. After few hours, slowly she opened her eyes and she was locked in a room which was filled with the dead bodies of her village people's.

Nakshatra Mala Dash

Nakshatra Mala Dash is a girl from Bhubaneswar Odisha, whose eyes are full of dreams and hopes. She has been a co-author in few anthologies. Her first e-book At Last you are mine is also available on Amazon.

The Perfect Change

A changed girl
I have changed a lot.
From being a girl who was afraid of darkness, now I have become a strong girl who can sit alone in darkness.
I have changed a lot.
From being a girl who cared too much, now I have become the most irresponsible girl who don't give a damn about anyone.
I have changed a lot.
From being a girl who pleaded everyone to stay, I have become the most egoistic girl, who now directly ask people to leave if they have a problem with me.
I have changed a lot.
From being an emotional fool, I have now become the most emotionless girl, you will ever see.
I have changed a lot.
From being chasing People's, I have now began to chase my dreams.
I have Changed a lot.

Reynu (Shradha Shintre)

Reynu (Shradha Shintre) is someone who writes In such a way that it connects right to the heart. She has been often accused of making people cry :). Yes she brings forth hidden emotions with her writing. She dabbles in different genres like short stories, articles but primary being Poetry. She's a graduate with her Specialisation being Psychology - this goes a long way in her understanding the psyche of Human nature, observing things around her and bringing it forth in her writing. Reading being her weakness and also her strength- she loves Romance Suspense and Self Help Books She Loves travelling and naturally runs a Travel Agency making people go where their Heart is!!!!

Children are her most loved characters In her Life. Anything children related is sure to make her smile. One will find a lot about them in her Writing!!

She has a YouTube channel and Instagram account by the name Poetry_Worth_Your _Time which helps her reach out to a vast audience!!! Do follow her:)

Choice

Many a time life will throw an unexpected curveball catching me by surprise
Forcing me to bend, fall and crumble
I know the choice is mine.... I choose to Rise.

On Many a day thing can go wrong, circumstances can try my patience, crawling traffic can hold me back
I can curse & scream or on someone else let out my steam
I know the choice is mine.... I choose to stay calm, smile and take things in my stride!!

Often situations seem unfair and I feel cheated. I worked so hard and did not get my due
I can get angry and think of ways to hurt and take Revenge...
I know the choice is mine.. I choose to forgive, it's not my place to God's job do...

As is wont, failure and Paucity I will encounter, Purse strings will be tight & all demands can't be met
I can cry, I can complain and despair, can blame birth, time and circumstances...
I know the choice is mine. I choose to be grateful, bide my time, work hard knowing times will change....

Human nature as it is, Relationships will strain. There will be petty fights and misunderstandings will try to stay
I can hold back, I can be mean, I can hold grudges & refuse to sway
I know the choice is mine... I Choose to Love, to embrace and let bygones be bygones and save the day...

The world can look dark, dreary and cold

The clouds can look overcast and the storm seems endless refusing to pass
I can get depressed and lonely and in myself withdraw.
I know the choice is mine... I Choose to look beyond- for the hidden Bright Rainbow, that subdued silver lining coz when in the Almighty I believe all the strife, problems and negativity will have to Cease!!!!

Samiksha Sharma

Samiksha Sharma belongs to Ganj Basoda, Madhya Pradesh is a social activist, mark her contribution in public welfare. Writing is her hobby; she is well confident and a versatile girl.

Seven Essence is her debut published work.

ठहराव से बदलाव तक

6 साल का रिलेशनशिप था हमारा, लोग कहते थे made for each other.. और हम दोनों मुस्कुरा दिया करते थे, लेकिन अचानक हमारे जीवन में कुछ संकट आया, उनका परिवार हमारे रिश्ते को स्वीकार नहीं कर सकता। उसने मुझे छोड़ दिया....
फ्यूचर प्लानिंग कर लिया था, घर की चार दीवारों का कलर, उसकी पसंद के पर्दे, सुबह की चाय मेरे हाथों की, गाड़ी छोटी या बड़ी किचन modular ya simple,अपने आप को पूरी तरीके से उसका कर बैठी थी यह 6 सालों में मेरी सारी जरूरत का ख्याल फिर वो रखता था।
16 जुलाई सुबह,
मां मेरे पास आए मेरे कमरे में, सर पर हाथ रखते हुए बोली भूल जाओ उस लड़के को.... और आमंत्रण पत्र मेरे हाथ में रखती हैं, ऐसा लगा जैसे कुछ छूट गया हो, कुछ टूट गया हो।
एक गहरा दर्द सीने में सांसे तेज और खुद को बस कमरे में बंद कर लिया!! वह चार दिवारी, वहां अंधेरा और सिर्फ उसकी यादें।
मां हर रोज खाने की थाली लाती और मैं मां से बोलती तुम क्यों आती हो चली जाओ.. "leave me alone!!"
यह कहकर मां को रुला देती थी, छोड़कर जाने पर उसके मां का प्यार भी कहीं खो गया। कभी हंसने लगती है तो कभी जोर जोर से रोने लगती, बेड के पीछे छुपी रहती। शायद पागल होने में और मुझ में महज एक सीडी का अंतर था । एक शाम खुद को इस दर्द से छुटकारा पाने की सोची थी, हां मर जाना आसान लग रहा था।पर एक शाम कुछ गजब हुआ,
हर रोज की तरह किड़किराने वाले मेरे पिता, एक लड़के के पीछे जिंदगी खराब करने वाले पानी देने वाले पिता, आज मेरे कमरे में थे छोटी सी मुस्कान और उनके बढ़ते कदम हाथों में खाने की थाली

थी, मैंने कहा आप क्यों आए हो ? मां कहां है?!! मुझ पर चिल्लाने आए हो क्या? उन्होंने कहा नहीं.. बात करनी है...
पराठे का पहला निवाला तोड़ अपने हाथों से मुझे खिलाया, मैं शांत थी और जोर जोर से रोने लगी।
कहां पापा सब खत्म हो गया अब.... मुझे दर्द हो रहा है, मुझे नहीं रहना।वह शांत थे, फिर बोले तुझे याद है जब पहली बार तू मंच पर गई थी और trophy आकर सीधा मेरे हाथों में थमा दी थी,
जब कक्षा दसवीं में राज्य स्तर पर तुम्हें पुरस्कृत किया गया, वह सबसे खूबसूरत पल।
जब तुमने लोगों के बीच कविता सुनाई और लोगों की भीड़ में तालियों की गूंज थी, उस भीड़ में मैं भी था।
वह मुझे वहां से उठा कर, drawing room तक ले गए, जहां मेरी यादें, मेरे हौसले, मेरा वजूद, कांच में रखी उन ट्रॉफियों और सर्टिफिकेट में कैद था।
उन्होंने मुझे खुद से रूबरू कराया, खो गई थी कहीं मैं मुझे फिर मुझसे मिलाया।
पिता ने फरिश्ता होने का फर्ज निभाया।

Raghav Chauhan

Raghav Chauhan (S/O Mr. Satyapal Singh & Mrs. Nisha Devi) is a young writer of Modern era. He was born on 6th July 1997 at Distt.Moradabad, UP.

He is 23 years old. He has started his journey of writing from Haridwar, A Holy Land of Uttarakhand. His early education was completed from Jaspur, U.S.N. Uttarakhand. His original name is Mr.Ramakant Singh.

He give more importance to "ORDINARY LIFE – HIGHER THOUGHT"in his life. He struggled a lot of his life by which many new Inspirations come to in his life.

He writes mostly spiritual quotes and articles On many topics such as " SPRITUAL KNOWLEDGE WOMEN EMPOWERMENT,NATURE, CULTURE AND CIVILIZATION, HUMAN LIFE, SOCIAL EVILS " etc.

He has also acted as Co-Author in 30 Anthologies under some publication likeBOOKSQUIRREL PUBLICATION,FLAIRS AND GLAIRS PUBLICATION, WISDOM PUBLICATION etc. He has currently featured in The On-zine Magazine for his article "Mental Stress (A serious problem of Modern era). Also titled as Compiler in 3 Anthologies under Booksquirrel Publication and FnG Publication.

Currently, he has honoured by many books of records such as OMG Book of records, Bravo International Book of records, Exclusive World Record, Vajra World Record for his anthology "Season's of Heart" by BookSquirrel Publication.
You can contact him on –
Instagram - @unprofessional_writer_raghav
Twitter - @Raghav Chauhan
Facebook – Truth of life @raghavchauhan2020
YQ App - @Raghav Chauhan

One Wish...

If I could have just one wish
I would wish to wake up everyday
To the sound of
 your breath on my neck.
your warmth lips on my cheek.
The touch of your fingers on my skin.
And the feel of your heart
 beating with mine.
Knowing that I could never find the feeling
With anyone other than you.

Ranajoy Biswas (Musafir)

काव्य की माया भोग से परे, है त्याग को समर्पित
त्यागी स्वयं ह्रदय अपना... शब्दरूप मे करता है अर्पित।
मुसाफिर

काव्य की इसी माया की खोज मे नबयुवक 'रणजय बिश्वास ऊर्फ मुसाफिर 'ने अपने बिद्यार्थी जीवन मे ही हिंदी एबं उर्दू साहित्य की कलाई थामी। शायरी, कविताएं, एबं छोटी रचनाओं के साथ साहित्य की यथा सम्भब सेवा की। अपने गृहनगर मे स्थित कोलकाता बिश्वविद्यालय के स्नातक 'मुसाफिर' अपनी छोटी रचनाओं के संकलन इंस्टाग्राम पे @musafir_ki_yaadein पर प्रकाशित भी करते है।

ज़माना यह, मुझे याद करेगा...

है सितम कुछ इतना नहीं,
की इस कदर मुझे बर्बाद करेगा...
मोहब्बत नहीं तो नफरत ही सही,
पर जमाना यह, मुझे याद करेगा।

है ठुकराया जमाने ने, तकदीर को मेरे,
पर, शाम नहीं मैं कोई जो यूं ही ढल जाऊं।
नामंज़ूरी भी भला किसी आग से कम कहा...
जो वक्त की आग में इस कदर जल जाऊं?

जलन भी तेरी, अब मुझे ज़ख्म देती नहीं
भला पत्थर दिल को तू क्या नाशाद करेगा?
मोहब्बत नहीं तो नफरत ही सही...
पर ज़माना यह, मुझे याद करेगा।

साहिल पे रहकर भी मैने,
गुफ्तगू गहराइयो से की...
सरहद ए चमन को छोड़ पीछे कही,
मोहब्बत उचाईयो से की।

शिकवा खुद ही से कही मुझे भी था...
यह ज़माना क्या मुझसे फ़रियाद करेगा?
मोहब्बत नहीं तो नफरत ही सही,
पर ज़माना यह, मुझे याद करेगा।

खूब मुबारक! ऐ वक़्त तुझे, की...
फज़र भी ना आया और शाम हो गई...
उजाले को छू लेने की वह तमन्ना मेरी,
कुछ यूं ही बदनाम हो गई।

पर है मंजूर, अब ऐ वक़्त मुझे...
वह हर एक, जो तू बेदाद करेगा।
मोहब्बत नहीं तो नफरत ही सही,
पर ज़माना यह, मुझे याद करेगा।

R. Sagarikaa

Sagarikaa, An aspiring writer who doesn't give a second thought before putting out her true opinions and feelings. She is pursuing her bachelors degree in Industrial design and is passionate about movies, music and cricket.

Overcome Challenges

Overcome Challenges, Everyday

My friend Shreya was one of the most positive people I had ever known. She was always in a good mood and always had something encouraging to say.

She was a manager at a restaurant. If her employee had a bad day, Shreya has always helped him to look on the positive side of the situation.

Shreya's attitude truly amazed me. So one day I asked her: "How can you be so positive all the time?".
She replied: "You see, every morning I tell myself that I have two choices for that day – to either be in a good mood or in a bad one. I try to choose the good one. And whenever something wrong happens, I can be sad and angry or I can learn from it instead. I choose to learn. Thus I choose the positive side of life".
I said: "It is not that easy". She replied: "Yes it is. Life is all about choices . You can choose how people or situations will affect your mood, your life".

One morning Shreya left the restaurant‘s back door open and was held up at gunpoint by three armed robbers. She tried to open the safe, but her hands shook due to nervousness and she slipped off the combination. So the robbers shot her. Fortunately, Shreya was quickly found and brought to the nearest hospital. After many hours of surgery and long intensive care, She was released home.

When I met her, I asked what her thoughts were during the robbery. "I thought that I should have locked the back door",

she replied. “Then, when I was lying on the floor, I remembered about my choices in this case: a choice to live and a choice to die. I chose to live.”

I asked if she was scared. She continued: “When they wheeled me into the emergency room and I looked at the faces of doctors, I got really scared. I knew that I needed to do something. So when the nurse asked me if I was allergic to anything, I replied “Yes”. Doctors and nurses stopped working as they waited for my answer. I took a deep breath and yelled, “Bullets”. They started laughing and I said: “My choice is to live, treat me as I am alive, not dead”.

Now Shreya is alive owing to skills of her doctors, however her amazing attitude played an important role too. I learned from her, that every day we should choose to live fully no matter what.

Sonali Gouda

Sonali, who rarely reads and writes. She seeks solace in smiles of all. She is not that great but definitely not like the rest.
To Everyone, have a great life ahead. Keep smiling.

The Endless Chase

The chase
I have been
following for years
is enough
to let me
feel the space
that is emerging
within - in between
you and me - us.
And the concern
of ours
regarding this
is quite
irrelevant as
Neither of us
is willing
to challenge
the emphasizing
and change it
into our
immense prosperity.
We with our all - might
may never know
that we are
leading to a
world of
indifference
full of ambivalence.

Constant Credence

Do you see what I get and sometimes choose to see
the clear, the blurred and sometimes few visions to unsee
Creation of what an amazing trace it would be
likely of a moment owning imperishable glee
when our feelings in upcoming time
may it be after some days, some years or some decades
would unite again and reach the ultimate
from nothing to everything - the whole thing
The reach to "all of this" from "none of this"
and leaving behind the preceedings
not worrying about the forthcomings
just the desire rooted deep within
fills me with all the belief therein.

Simmy

Chirping girl , simmy belongs from Ludhiana,punjab .she loves to pen emotions and reality.she writes to express herself. Her Instagram handle is @loovvee_feelings.

My Love

My love
We are so apart just sixty one kilometres;
a journey of one hour,
yet, i choose to be with you.

I have created a paradise of glee,
embellished with memories of togetherness,
build a home for our happiness.

the reason of my happiness,
the reason of my smile ,
the foundation of my change; is you.

A change that uplifted me for myself,
a change that encouraged me for self love,
a change that disclosed a new me in myself.

I love, life, laugh and show concern,
I desire , admire ,inspire ; my love.

Being together becoming a challenge,
but i am concerned about your desire,
and the dreams you respire.

My chase for true love has completed,
I found answers of all questions,
my treasure , my love, my world
all ends at you.

The moment you become part of my life,
I never planned; it was all destined
all sudden, yet impactful

all planned, yet so perfect.

Perhaps, our story is drenched in love,
and i want to swim across,
to be with you forever.

Prashant Tyagi

Prashant loves to talk about books, music, food, spirituality and everything else. Writing has been something of an emotional release for him, but like all good things he doesn't like to share it always because it's very much of a personal thing. Rab ki mehr h uske paas and also the answer why joey doesn't share food.

Nostalgia

It was one of my new friends who joked today if she can die as I don't love her, what did I reply? No please don't die but carry the burden you are to eternity, like I do. I don't it and I can't lie anymore.

It's just the void inside of me that does not want to stay calm it wants to scream, to hug, to see one last time what I won't ever have.

Yeah, this is how okay it is these days for me.

To see those words one last time, she said she does not cry now but how to explain I don't even feel. I love but I don't smile I can't cry but I don't feel sad. I can be ab Ek late at nights without having a thing in my mind I have the cried after that day I was on the verge of bruising the gift of breathing by my parents.

Maybe I don't want to, maybe I don't want to cry because it will take evade the last piece, I am left with the last piece of the beautiful image I made so dearly. It will be taken away and would never be given back. Maybe someday I won't even remember the person who broke my heart on my birthday asking me not to play the birthday card. Diet until that day when I will forget about what I had and on that person's existence. Maybe I will be a different person and I desperately want that someday to be today, trust me on this the person is not what is hurting me, the memories are. I feel like a piece of me is taken away and I can't even be myself, cause even if I will figure out to hold myself together it can never be the same. I don't believe in fairy tales anymore. I don't find happiness in eating bangali rosogolla on first dates. These three words don't slip out of my mouth anymore. Now I don't see myself planning stupid future with anyone. I don't it seems that I will run away from here while holding someone's hand, I don't want someone to talk to my

mother on call how to hang out with my dad. I am trying though but I am still sitting on the exact same space where everything happened. I am still desperately running in my room nothing have changed, everything has changed.
How it was changed me! I want, I respect and love my parents more and I want to be there for my niece and nephews more. I listen to all my friends you must think oh! you have changed for the better! Have I?
I still want to see you but I don't trust myself now I understand what is the true essence of being burnt alive of getting a papercut. Now I don't need your hug to sleep or maybe that's what I want to believe that I don't need your warm embrace.
Maybe I will dream again and it's the sad part that that's my only dream right now to feel and see dreams which I believe in and you know what I don't even believe in myself.

Vishakha Malukani (Morika)

Vishakha Malukani belongs to Indore. She loves reading & writing. She being an introvert soul loves to pen down her Feelings. She is currently pursuing MA Psychology. She is a published author her second book will be published soon.

Journey Of Chasing Love

At the age of 2, she didn't know what chasing is she was jaan of her family. As she grew up, she realised love is not meant for everyone.

At the age of 4, she chased for love of her father after her sibling came into this world as her father always wanted a boy child.

At the age of 6, she chased for the love and attention of her other family members after her cousins were born before them, she was the only child in the family dearer to everyone.

At the age of 8, she chased for the love of her sibling after he made new friends in colony.

At the age of 12, she chased for the love of her best friend, after her best friend got a new best friend.

At the age of 16, she chased for the love of her school crush who always liked her best friend.

This journey of chasing love scared her so much that she started staying away from the people she always loved whole-heartedly

At the age of 21, she fell for someone whom she called her boyfriend who made her feel & made her believe that she deserves to be loved but unfortunately with time he too changed.

Again, she was left heart broken.

But this time she learned that: -

“She needs to stop chasing the wrong ones because right ones may be waiting to be chased & moved on happily".

Then finally at the age of 25, she met love of her life who loved her so much and changed her mentality about love, changed her fear to confidence her insecurities to calmness & her self-doubt to self-love.

Sudipta

Student of history and archaeology; passionate about music, loves nature and animals; vegan and antinatalist. She hails from Assam.

Anhedonia

Nothing feels good anymore
Every moment I keep shedding tears
And cry my heart out.
I crave for love and affection
As I've never received from anybody.
I'm breaking into pieces inside
And I wish someone by my side
But this world seems to be unkind.
I cry, shout, wail and weep more
Pondering and reflecting my life
How my parents abandoned me,
How my friends back-stabbed me,
How my love destroyed me,
How I trusted strangers then
And they too deceived me.
Now I'm left alone with my anhedonia
And nothing to lift myself up
For this world has torn me down
And made me a soulless corpse.

The Stoic

To what more pain shall I succumb?
My heart is already numb.
My childhood saw many dreams,
But now my soul only screams
In stillness and silence.
But, I'm abound in patience
Because I've become a stoic.

Death

Losing myself and decaying
I've become a changed person;
There's nothing to hold on to anymore.
Counting each day as passes by
And waiting for my body to perish
While realizing my days are numbered
I crave for the old me.
But my soul is completely crushed
And I'm already dead.

Ankit Acharya

अंकित आचार्य (साहब) का जन्म-26 /जनवरी /1993, गंज बासौदा जिला विदिशा मध्यप्रदेश में हुआ था, ये हिंदी एवं संस्कृत भाषा में लिखते है, इनकी शिक्षा संस्कृत महाविद्यालय भोपाल से हुई है!

"हकीक़त ही लिखेंगे ओर बात चुनिन्दा रख्खेगें
मरने नहीं देंगे मुझे मेरे शब्द जिन्दा रख्खेंगे
शब्दो के सामने कुछ दिखा ही नहीं
हजार कोशिशे की में बिका ही नहीं
सबको पड़ने के बाद याद आया
मेने खुद पे तो कुछ लिखा ही नही"
[@ankit.acharya3633] पे आप इन्हें पढ़ सकते है।

शुरुआत करो

शुरुआत करो शुरुआत करो
तुम नए युग की शुरुआत करो
लक्ष्य बनाओ जीवन पथ पर
पाने की शुरुआत करो !!
क्या खोया क्या पाया हमने
छोड़कर इन सब बातों को
लक्ष्य रखो सूरज पाने का
भूल के काली रातों को!!
बिना लक्ष्य कोरे कागज हो
कोरा ही रह जाओगे
बिना कमान तीर हो तुम
कोई अक्ष भेद नहीं पाओगे!!
खौफ हटा कर कुछ खोने का
पाने की कसम उठाओ तो
मंजिल खड़ी वहां फ़ेलाए
रस्ते पर तुम आओ तो!!
हार नहीं होती जीवन में
जब तक माना जाए ना
जीत नहीं सकते खुद से ही
गर मन में ठाना जाए ना!!
क्या करे क्या कर सकते है
गीत अगर ये गाओगे
गाते गाते इसी गीत को
खुद मे गुम हो जाओगे !!
इतिहास उठाकर देख लो तुम
संघर्ष छपे नजर आते हैं
लग जाते जिन पन्नों पर
पन्ने भी अमर कर जाते हैं!!

जिस वक्त लक्ष्य की पहली सीढ़ी
कदम तेरे चढ़ जाएंगे
हंसने वाले ए चेहरे
मुस्कुराहट में बदल लिये जाएंगे!!

Santosh Sharma

Santosh Sharma hails from Ganj Basoda, Madhys Pradesh, is a government employee keen his intrest in writing this writeup is his second published work.

He contributed in the book "elysian an eye shower" as a co-author.

बदलाव जरूरी है

लक्ष्य को अभेद कर,
तुम जान अपनी झोक दो।
डगमगाए अगर कदम,
तो खुद को पल भर रोक लो।
रोक के तुम कदम मन से ये जान लो,
राह क्यों थी, ये चुनी,
ये प्रश्न खुद ही जांच लो।
अगर चुनौती से डरे ,
तो दर्द क्या उठाओगे।
दर्द से जो डर गए
तो लक्ष्य कैसे पाओगे।
बदलाव जरूरी है,
बातों में।
बदलाव जरूरी है,
राहों में।
पर
स्थिरता की ज्योत जरूरी
लक्ष्य के चुनाव में।
बढ़े चलो बहाव में,
लक्ष्य ही विराम है,
तभी तो फिर आराम है।

Manisha Shrivastava

Manisha srivastava hills from Ganj Basoda Madhya Pradesh. She has her interest in writing. This writeup is her first published work.

She says:

निराशा से उबरें समय की कद्र करें जीवन अनमोल है शुरुआत कभी भी करें

समय शुरुआत का जीवन की किसी भी अवस्था में हो सकता है।

समय

रेत को मुट्ठी में बंद कर मैं कस कर पकड़ बैठी थी लेकिन अंतराल के बाद एक भी कण हाथ में रुक न सका समय भी इसी कण के साथ आवृत बढ़ता रहा मैं कब बचपन से युवा और कब बुढ़ापे की दहलीज पर पैर रखकर बैठ गयी बस यही से शायद मेरी जीवन यात्रा प्रारंभ हुई।

अब मेरे पास समय पर्याप्त है पर समय काटने के समाधाम में मेरा मत नहीं लगता मेरा मन लौट कर फिर पुनरावृत्ति के लिए व्याकुल है।

घर के छोटे बड़े सभी व्यस्त हैं समय, मैंने बताया न किसी के पास नहीं है। समय को कोई बांध नहीं पाया मैं समय को रोकना नहीं चाहता था पर, आज समय है और मैं चाहता हूं कोई मुझे समय दे दे या समय को आगे बढ़ा दे।

पर इस हमें समय को आगे बढ़ाने की सोच में उस समय बदलाव आया, जब मैंने टीवी में वृद्ध आश्रम में जीवन बिता रहे बुजुर्गों को देखा कैसे जीवन की शाम को गैरों के साथ भी बता रहे थे। मैं तो अपनों के बीच थी, फिर इसी सोच ने मुझे प्रेरणा दी , मैंने जीवन की दिशा बदलने की ठानी । एक सुबह मैंने नई शुरुआत की । पार्क में पहुंच कुछ पुराने चेहरे मिले तो ऊर्जा का संचार हुआ । फिर मैंने समय के साथ रुकना नहीं चलना शुरू कर दिया। बच्चों के साथ समय बिताना मैंने शुरू कर दिया। मेरी रुचि जो दब गई थी उसकी धूल साफ कि। आज मुझे जीवन की सांझ में सभी समय देने लगे क्योंकि समय की कीमत जो समझता है सभी उसी को समय देते हैं॥

Dr. Chandramani Goswami

Dr. Chandramani Goswami is professionally an educator, an active researcher and published many international journals (https://scholar.google.com/citations?user=E24RGv4AAAAJ&hl=en). He did his Ph. D. in Mechanical Engineering. He is also a poet, writer and author of "Elysian an Eye Shower" (which you can access from here: https://www.amazon.in/Elysian-Eye-Shower-Sumit-Sharma/dp/B08J1F18FJ). He lives in the pink city of Jaipur, India.

Prints Are Immortal

Choose ...
To stand for self
Choose ...
To lay a change.
A change ...
Towards the right.
A change ...
To feel delight.
A change ...
To reach so high.
A change
To touch the sky.
A change
To its positive side.
A change
Which brought a concern,
Concern which is nourished by care.
Care to get ready for challenges.
Challenges to chase and fight.
fight which is set for right.
right for self,
which will mark a stamp.
Stamp of winning.
This winning will forever be remembered.
Your footprints towards the win will make it
never closure.

Akhil Prakash

Akhil Prakash is a software Engineer by profession. He hails from Calicut district of Kerala. Apart from his work, he is passionate about writing blogs, doing social work and running marathons

Challenges Will Keep Knocking

Challenges will keep knocking at each stage of your life.
You just choose to stay light.
Choose to stay right,
until you see the light,
at the end of the tunnel.
If you fall down, get up and move on.
Crawl like a worm,
fly like a bird,
swim like a fish,
Stay till the end.

Challenges will keep knocking at each stage of your life.
You just choose to stay light.
Don't be afraid of night.
Darkness will soon end.
Light shall soon prevail.
Life is a roller coaster ride,
with some scary ups and downs.
You just choose to stay light,
to make it straight.
You will soon see the light

Chieag L Sagar

Chirag L Sagar is a 2nd year MBBS student studying at Srinivas Institute of Medical Sciences and Research Centre,Mangalore. His hobbies are poetry, reading - books,novels, autobiographies,philately, listening to songs,sports like cricket and badminton,cooking. He is a medico by profession and a writer by passion. His dream is to become an Oncologist and a successful writer.

Instagram : @chirag_cls18 Facebook : Chirag LSagar

Quotes

1. You alone can create your path to a bright future

2. When in confusion, choose what your soul feels right

Niharika N Jain

Niharika is a writer from tumkur,Karnataka.She also writes in kannada and hindi. Niharika is an engineering student by profession. She believes that words are the best way to Express our inner feelings

Way To A Beautiful Life...

Learn to choose the things which help you make your dreams come true.
Create your own indentity by achieving the glory of success in your life.
Adjust to the changes that comes in life, because life always doesn't remain the same.
Have concern about your health because health is wealth.
Try accept challenges and complete the in time.
Chase your dreams , because if you leave them behind , you will also stay behind in your life.
Try to close or finish your work in given time.

The 7C's Of Life

Choose what you love,
Create what you aspire,
Change for what you believe,
Challenge for what you dream,
Chase for what you live,
Concern for which is important,
Close what you don't need.

Mariya Sadaf

Hello everybody. So, meet this budding writer Ms. Mariya Sadaf. She has recently started up with her writings. Right now she's doing BA. And she belongs to Allahabad, India. She has recently got her story published. And she's also a very good speaker. Hope you'll love her work.

The Show Must Go On.!

The Show Must Go On.! No matter how bad/good our performance is on the platform of life, no matter how the people reacted, no matter what you received- standing ovation or tomatoes or eggs thrown at you.

All that matters is that the choices you come up with, the creativity you add so as to make it more beautiful, the changes you do so as to make it more unique and different from others. The concern you have towards the choice you made, the challenges you go through, and the way you chase it no matter what others said and how they reacted. And finally, the way you close it.

You have been sent into this world with so much of uniqueness ie. your fingerprint, DNA, your way of taking things, your thoughts, your views. And your ideas. We come up with a lot of thoughts and we try to make it more beautiful and implement it in our life. This doesn't mean that every wild notion we come up with is genius. But we should appreciate it and should not let any idiot talk over it. If you feel something, something you feel is genuinely good and something you want to do. Something which means something to you-- try to do it. Because I think you can only do your best when you are implementing your own ideas because you'll never allow yourself to get down. Do that something according to your own idea don't let others disturb your plan. And then take pride in whatever you have done. Don't cry or feel low if it turns out to be disastrous, coz sweetheart Amby few use their brain and a few take chances of living life according to their own will you are smarter and stronger than you think. Be very confident for what you did. It's your life, your ideas will act like "cherry on the cake".

Even if your plans don't workout accordingly, you'll get experience in return and you'll be more careful and confident the next time you'll attend to do that something again.

There are some people who live for others, caring for them and giving up on their choices to make others happy and in their happiness, they find themselves to be very lucky and content. But, once just try to work for your happiness too and give yourself a chance to feel that much lucky that you are able to make yourself feel special.

We make a lot of choices regarding studies, career, relationships, etc. And sometimes in trying to give our best in these we sometimes compromise with our happiness. I've seen people working or living life under someone else's rules and regulations. That's not fair. Don't do this to your own self. All I want to say is that live your life cherishes each and every moment. Make plans follow them set your goals no matter what it is for others. The thing that matters the most is your happiness no one is going to provide you the happiness which you can do to yourself.

I, usually follow my own terms but yes this is the fact that I've also compromised with a few dreams, which I wanted to follow. Just because I'm very much afraid of W's and H (when, where, why, who, what and how). I've never struggled in my life except with these questions. And I think so that most of us struggle with the same.

In my case I made and I still make a lot of choices. My father being very concerned about my marks which is the biggest drawback I go through. I don't like remembering dates and going to examination hall and writing those stuff. I wanted to create something of my own. And each day I was discovering my own self. And the conclusion that I've been sent into this world for a very special purpose and that's to do something good and great fir myself and for the ones who

know me. I didn't like to work as a slave under someone for the sake of money. And as I was trying to understand myself, I came to know that I am a good speaker. People were appreciating it and we're loving the way I speak except my dear parents. I know they were also very proud of this talent of mine but again those digits came into my way reminding my parents that just speaking skills will not lead your daughter to a bright future.

Anyways I kept working on it as I know how much good I feel in doing this. So, I never gave up on this despite of being questioned again and again that, "What are you doing? Why are you doing? Where it will lead you to?" Ignoring these questions and sometimes giving rude replies... arguing with them rather telling them that they don't have enough capability to understand my idea, my dreams. And it went on....

During a talent show I shared words with a man not very different from me Mr. Aman Pratap Singh who gave me an offer to work with him. What work I didn't know. But all he told me is that, I talk too much and I can even write books. So, this special person saw something special in me and invited to attend a webinar regarding Network Marketing.

As soon as the session ended, I was like that this is the platform where I can represent me and my ideas. During this I came across allot of people who were not very different from me. Like all of them were concerned about their happiness and through that how they can also make others happy. So, there were people who were also struggling with the very same problem as mine, the W's and H struggle. People like Ms. Aakriti, Ms. Shruti, Mr. Shivam Saxena, Mr. Atul Gupta and many more innocent people. So, after sharing words with them I decided to follow their footprints as they have experienced how to overcome those problem and issues. I decided to work with them and to explore myself in a better way.

•The first step seems to be easy where I chose to be a Network Marketer.

• The second step was to create new ideas regarding the choice I made. I created alot of wishes through which I can make money and name. I wrote down my short-term plans as well as long term ones.

• The third was to bring changes.
And the change starts with you. And so it happened in my case too. I also developed some new rules and tries to implement it.

• The fourth was that how much I was concerned about my choice. I was working on it during the beginning.

• Now comes challenge where I went through ups and downs. There were times I broke down but there were people who were able to piece me back again. The most difficult task was to share this to my parents. My plan was to give them a surprise with the income I'll receive. The toughest challenge was to go through the word NO during inviting people. They were like "Why are you there in Network Marketing?" And there I just use to say it's my life, my dream, my rules. You are no one to interrupt. It was easy to say this to the people I don't care what they think of me. But when the same question was asked from the special ones, I used to run short of words. With tears in my eyes, I was just able to say that one day you'll be congratulating me for what I chose as I was confident enough that yes, I will do something very great.

•The sixth was the way i chase it, was a bit different. I was crazy for it. The meetings which took place I used to attend all no matter how and what the situations were.

• The last how I closed the choice I made. To be honest I never ended because I know I understand that things take time.

No matter what ever you choose in your life, the thing that matters the most is how you are carrying it in and living it. If you give up you prove that the choice you made was not that good. All I want to convey is don't give up. Life will be hard, there will be turmoil's but only for making you stronger, more confident and to turn you in the best version. My mentors, my leaders have always taught me to get up and this time to be stronger than before. Wait for the right person dude. Let the right person come to you.
Today the attitude I have is because of the right humans I have in my life. Be very strict in choosing people because the environment matters the most.
Be kind to you and then only you can be kind to others.
I have been broken many times but the people in my life have made me feel stronger. In the words of Mr. Akshay K. Agarwal, "We are here to solve the same issue 100 times and not to laugh at your failures. We are here to support you and to help you in leading the life you dreamt. But the only person who will never give up on you is you yourself."
So, cherish your presence celebrate your life as you don't know how special ur presence is. Choose wisely, create ideas, change the mentality, be concerned, accept the challenges, chase them as crazy people, then finally after the results close it but learn from it !!!

Flairs and Glairs, a platform by a student for the students. We are esteemed youth struggling to carve out our path for our future and we follow a basic mindset Since everyone is not born with all-round skills. Joining hands with people who are born to execute it with perfection is the best way to evolve. Self-Evolution is the need of the hour but, evolving as a community is what we strive for. The initiative as kickstarted by, Founder- Mr. Shubham Shah with the motive to utilize the skillset and talent of writing has now a team of 10+ people who are actively participating into newer forms of learning and discovering talents among youngsters. We Provide platform and services like Publishing opportunities, Open mics, Workshops, Hands-on training. Operating with Brand Name of Flairs and Glairs (Publication House), we offer the chance of elevating a passionate writer to an esteemed author With Brand name Teekhe Zasbaaat. We bring to you an opportunity to get accustomed with the Public Speaking and Presenting of Thoughts along with regular challenges to brush up your inking spirit. The newest initiative to extend our services we introduced in a new writing Platform- The Glittering Fables and Ink Over Tears.

We Choose to Fly Like A Falcon than to be

a Leg Pulling Crab.

To Know More: Infoline – 7781900870
Mail Us At-
flairsandglairs@gmail.com / info@flairsandglairs.in
Or Visit is at
www.flairsandglairs.com / www.flairsandglairs.in
Social Handles- @flairsandglairs @teekhezasbaaat

www.ingramcontent.com/pod-product-compliance
Ingram Content Group UK Ltd.
Pitfield, Milton Keynes, MK11 3LW, UK
UKHW022004190726
13853UKWH00004B/1734